D1622156

The Adventures of Puppy

A Gentleman Rabbit

The Adventures of Puppy

A
Gentleman
Rabbit

Four Rhyming Tales

Dennis Kyte

SMITHMARK

This edition published in 1998 by
SMITHMARK Publishers,
a division of U.S. Media Holdings, Inc.,
115 West 18th Street, New York, NY 10011.

SMITHMARK books are available for bulk purchase for sales promotion and premium use.
For details write or call the manager of special sales,
SMITHMARK Publishers,
115 West 18th Street, New York, NY 10011,
212–519–1300.

Designed by Melanie Random & Lisa Vaughn

ISBN: 0–7651–0857–7

Printed in Hong Kong

10 9 8 7 6 5 4 3 2 1

Library of Congress Catalog Card Number: 98–60958

this book belongs to:

_____

_____

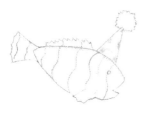

contents

Puppy Gets Around

Puppy is a rabbit who leaves

his cottage and thinks, *how shall I go?*

I can take to the air.

I can take to the sea.

I can take to the road,

but I must take my key.

For when I go far, as far as I roam,

I never forget that

it's best coming home.

Puppy in the Garden

Puppy is a rabbit who sleeps in his

garden and gets up with the sun.

The flowers need fiddling

and when that's all done,

The bushes need whacking

and the vegetables, sacking.

And when the sun sets on

a patch of paper hearts,

it's time to light the fire

and make the carrot tarts.

Then sweet lettuce sandwiches,

crispy and cool,

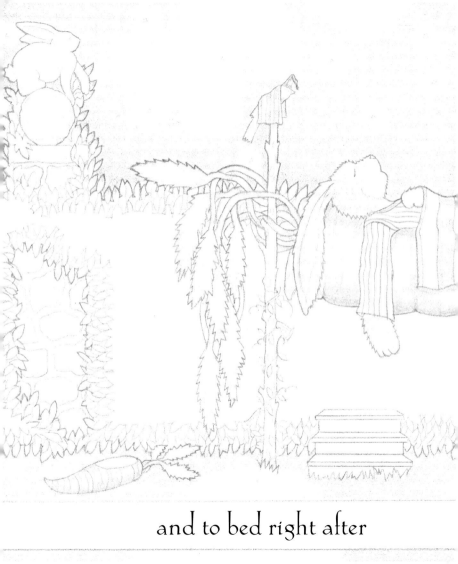

and to bed right after

...for that is the rule.

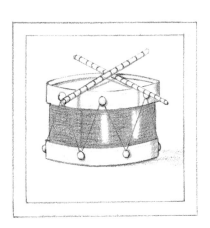

Puppy Plays a Song

Puppy is a rabbit whose

garden grows and grows,

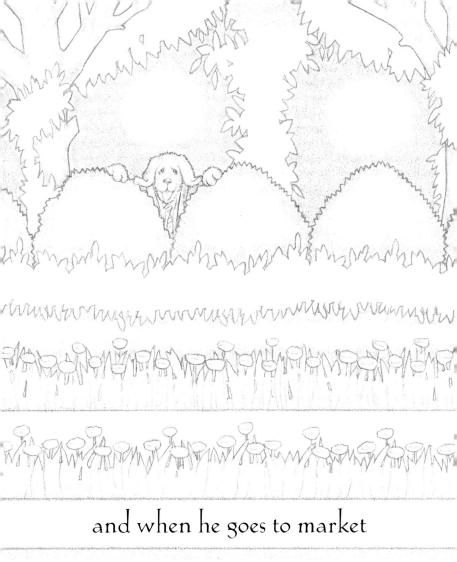

and when he goes to market

he plays a song he knows.

He plays it for a dandy dog

who likes to bark along.

He plays it for three silly hens

who like to cluck the song.

He plays it for a circus duck

who has a blue balloon.

The friends all go to market

and share the work to do,

and all join in and sing the song

when all their work is through!

Puppy Tidies Up

Puppy is a rabbit

who is very, very neat,

but sometimes his cottage

needs tidying up.

That's when he

sings this little song:

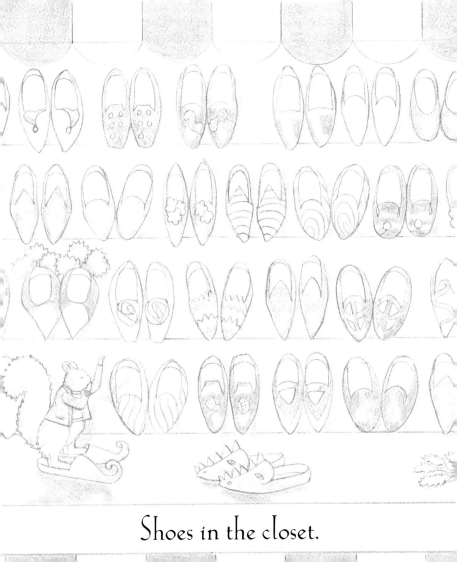

Shoes in the closet.

Sweaters on the shelf.

Bed's all made.

I did it myself!

Puppy is a rabbit

who is very, very neat.